Jeet and Fudge

Fun at the
WATER PARK!

by Amandeep S. Kochar

PAW PRINTS PUBLISHING

pawprintspublishing.com

Book and Cover Design by Maureen O'Connor
Art Direction by Nishant Mudgal
Illustrated by Weaverbird Interactive

Edited by Bobbie Bensur and Alison A. Curtin

English Paperback ISBN: 978-1-22318-350-3
English Library ISBN: 978-1-51826-298-2
English eBook ISBN: 978-1-22318-351-0

Published by Paw Prints Publishing
PawPrintsPublishing.com
Printed in Ashland, OH, USA

It's Animal Shelter Day at the water park!
Dad, Jeet, and Fudge are there to help sign up foster families.

It's been epic!

After a while, the three are ready to take a break and play in the water!

"Okay. We have a half hour," says Dad. "What will we ride first?"

"How about we go on the biggest slide?"

"Okay, Bappu!" says Jeet.

In line, a little girl taps Jeet on the shoulder. "We lost our new dog's chew toy. It looks like a carrot!" she says.

"Oh! Well, we haven't seen it, but we'll help look," says Jeet.

But wait! Where is Fudge running to?

Do you see what she sees?

She's found the chew toy! "Thanks, Fudge!" says the little girl. Jeet is proud of Fudge.

Everyone is happy. So Jeet, Fudge, and Dad get back in line to wait their turn.

But they don't have much time before they need to go back to the volunteer table!

But. . .

someone else needs their help!

The lady is thankful they saved her money from flying away.

But it means that Jeet, Fudge, and Dad have even less time to play.

"Let's try again!" says Jeet.

But before they can hop on the ride, they hear it. . .

a great, big sob.

"Are you okay?" Jeet asks the sad little boy.

"We don't have any more tickets," sniffs the boy. "And I really wanted to go on that ride with my dad."

"Come on, Bappu. Let's just go back to the volunteer table," says Jeet.

"Wait!" says the ticket taker. "I've watched you and your puppy help so many people today.

That deserves a pass to the front for at least one quick ride!"

"Really?" says Jeet. "Thank you!"
"Have fun!" the ticket taker tells them.

And so, the forever friends—Jeet and Fudge—finally get to ride the big waterslide.
And it's epic!

THE BENEFITS OF VOLUNTEERING

Volunteering can be a very positive experience for children of all ages. Here are some of the benefits:

👍 **Teaching Appreciation** – volunteering can increase a child's appreciation of what they have and make them more grateful.

👍 **Building Empathy** – volunteering can expose children to people from different backgrounds, helping them widen their perspective and create bonds that can foster empathy for all types of people.

👍 **Building Self-Esteem** – volunteering can allow children to learn new skills and develop their strengths, which can give them a sense of purpose, independence, and self-efficacy.

👍 **Creating a Better Community** – working as a volunteer in one's own community can increase feelings of belonging and helps make the community a better place for everyone.

👍 **Developing Important Skills** – collaborating with others to bring about change and reach goals can improve social skills, communication skills, responsibility, and commitment.

Did You Know?

One of the core tenets of the Sikh religion is being of service to others without expecting anything in return. This is known as *seva*. Sikhs believe that all human beings are equal and that, when given the opportunity, we must help those who are less fortunate. Jeet exemplifies this Sikh value at the water park when he helps the girl find the lost dog toy, returns the money to the lady who lost it, and gives his two tickets to the little boy and his dad. Jeet also demonstrates selfless service when he volunteers at the animal shelter event.